Colonial Klaus

in Thomas Jefferson's House

by Laura A. Macaluso

Illustrated by
Lynden A. Godsoe

THOMAS JEFFERSON'S

Poplar Forest

Thomas Jefferson's Poplar Forest
1542 Bateman Bridge Road
Forest, Virginia 24551
www.poplarforest.org

www.mascotbooks.com

Colonial Klaus

This Mascot Books hardcover edition printed 2019.

For more information, please contact:
Mascot Books
620 Herndon Parkway #320
Herndon, VA 20170
info@mascotbooks.com

Library of Congress Control Number: 2018956181

CPSIA Code: PRT0319A
ISBN-13: 978-1-64307-391-0

Printed in the United States

Inside covers:
Map of Poplar Forest drawn by Thomas Jefferson
circa 1809. Photo by J.H. Ogborne, Ph.D.

Dedication

This tale of a little dog named Klaus introduces young readers to a real story that happened more than two hundred years ago—and that is the story of the people, both black and white, who lived and worked in the octagonal house designed by Thomas Jefferson, and on the 5,000-acre plantation that surrounded the house and helped support the Jefferson family.

Jefferson had owned the plantation called Poplar Forest since 1773, when he inherited the land—and people—from his new father-in-law. He kept the plantation running and visited sporadically, most famously in 1781, when the British chased him out of Richmond, across the Commonwealth to his first house Monticello, and finally down to Poplar Forest. There, living in the overseer's house, Jefferson wrote most of his only book, *Notes on the State of Virginia*. Jefferson did not begin building his own house at Poplar Forest until 1806, in the last years of his presidency, but, when he did, he took all of the knowledge learned over a lifetime of reading, study, and travel to design a perfect octagon with a skylight over the cube dining room (the dimensions of the room are 20′ x 20′ x 20′). Before Jefferson inherited it, Poplar Forest had been named for the abundance of tulip poplars that grew on the land. During the years of Jefferson's ownership of the house and the land, more than 200 enslaved African Americans—men, women, and children—made an impact on Poplar Forest, providing essential value to the Jefferson family in many different ways. While Klaus is a real dog who lives in Lynchburg today, Billy and Hannah Hubbard and Burwell Colbert were real people who toiled at Poplar Forest more than two hundred years ago. This book is dedicated to them.

The Tri-Corn Hat

The little dog—he was a long-haired **dachshund**, if you must know, very close to the ground with black silky fur and front feet that turned outward—popped his head up at the scene before him. Just a moment ago, the dachshund had been on a walk with his owner, a tall man with brown hair and glasses with whom he rode in a little silver car that had no roof, allowing the little dog to sniff the air with ease. Together they often walked the **allée** of mulberry trees and under crooked branches of tulip poplars, which were two hundred years old.

Now, he found that his owner was nowhere to be seen and that the air smelled different somehow. He couldn't quite put his paw on it, but something had changed since he followed the rabbit into his hole at the base of one of the old trees. Klaus couldn't help it—he was a dachshund after all, and dachshunds were bred to chase other small animals. His long snout, short legs, and sausage-like body were made for tunneling in the earth. But, this time, it seemed, his instinct had gotten him into trouble.

Where exactly was he, wondered the little dog as he peered through the tall grass, and why was he wearing this grey wool hat? Dachshunds don't wear hats, especially hats with a feather in the brim. Nevertheless, he had come out of the rabbit hole with the hat and he wasn't going to leave it behind.

Summer Grass

A gentle breeze was blowing, causing the grass to sway back and forth, and it tickled the little dog's nose and stood much taller than he, sometimes closing in above his head. Klaus pushed the tall grass aside with his snout and made his way forward, enjoying the sweet smell of the earth and sunshine filling the air. It was **intoxicating.** He stood there for just a minute or two, feeling the sun warm his black coat.

His quiet **reverie** was soon broken when Klaus felt the earth tremble, and heard a sound in the distance that was unusual to him—feet hitting the ground much harder and louder than his own four little paws could do. With a hop, he pushed forward through the grass and stumbled upon a dirt road.

Standing still for a moment to catch his breath, Klaus watched in wonder as two horses pulling a carriage came into view and proceeded to stop right next to him. An older man with ginger hair streaked with white leaned over and exclaimed, "Hello, curious **visitant!**" with a generous smile. Two young women sat next to him and they smiled too, and giggled just a bit—the little dog was so close to the ground that they could hardly see him over the side of the carriage.

The Curious Visitant

"I'm surprised you found me here, curious visitant! I come to Poplar Forest only a few times a year—how fortunate that I chose this time to come, allowing me to meet someone who still remembers the great 'Spirit of '76!'" With those words, the man took off his own wool hat and bowed his head towards the little dog.

Klaus had never seen such courtly manners—certainly his owner with the silver car was a nice fellow, but his manners were far from what he was witnessing here! The little dog decided to do the same and bowing his snout just a bit, Klaus took off the wool hat with a feather in his brim, which again made the girls giggle.

Their laughs caught the man's attention, and he cleared his throat. "May I introduce my granddaughters, Ellen and Cornelia? And, I, my short-legged friend, am Thomas Jefferson, your humble servant!" The tall, ginger-haired man stepped out of the carriage and bent over quite a ways to reach down to the little dog, shaking hand-to-paw.

"I see from your dog tag that your name is Colonial Klaus!" said Mr. Jefferson. "Well, judging from your **pedigree** you are of German **ancestry**, so I must ask, are you an **acquaintance** by chance of the Baron von Steuben, who helped to train our American soldiers during the **Revolutionary War?**"

Klaus really didn't know whom Mr. Jefferson was talking about—the only baron he had ever heard anything about was the Red Baron, who fought Snoopy in World War I, but, that was another story for another time. He wagged his fluffy tail
just the same in order to please the man, as any dog would.

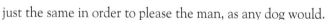

An Invitation to Supper

The sun was hot out there on the dirt road, and Ellen and Cornelia began looking a little **peaked**. Mr. Jefferson turned to Colonial Klaus and said, "We are going to my octagonal house for a little rest and reading in the library this afternoon. And, although I value my private time here at Poplar Forest, something tells me that you could use a little food—and maybe a sip of beer or wine from my wine cellar, too. Please join us at 3 p.m. for some **plantation fare** made by my cook Hannah Hubbard."

Klaus, being a dog that never turned down a free scrap of food (unless it was dry toast with no butter) realized he was hungry, and the girls were looking at him expectantly, so he barked his **assent** yes! He smiled back at them, his little black lips parting to show just a little of his pink tongue and very white teeth (although some people don't know this, dogs can smile when they are happy).

Mr. Jefferson then tipped his hat again at Klaus—who had somehow traveled back to a time just after the Colonial era, an era of courtly manners and talk of Revolution and mid-afternoon suppers—and picked up the reins, slapping them against the carriage so the horses moved on.

Tomahawk Creek

As the carriage moved away from him, becoming smaller and smaller in the distance, other sounds were softly filling the air. Colonial Klaus's nose and his ears gave him the direction in which to walk. Ears are a very fine feature of a long-haired dachshund, although his short stance meant he was always very close to the ground, and his ears often picked up pieces of grass and other unwelcome things, like nettles. Finding a narrow path off of the dirt road, the little dog followed the voices that traveled over the grasses, until he came upon a creek.

There was clear water running over rocks and the red Virginia soil, and Colonial Klaus lapped up a few mouthfuls. A turtle sat sunning itself on a nearby rock, its shell a **geometric** pattern of yellow and green, but Klaus paid the creature no attention (turtles weren't very fun, because when you chased them, they pulled their head and legs into their shells and became **immobile**, which is kind of boring to a dachshund who likes to chase things).

The water was cool and delicious on his pink tongue, but as he stood there lapping, he noticed out of the corner of his eye that someone was standing farther down the creek, splashing the cold water on his face and washing his hands. Looking harder, the little dog **discerned** this person was a young man, and that he was filling a wooden bucket before turning away from the creek to walk back up over the hill. The little dog, who was, after all, a curious visitant, took after the young man, keeping a safe distance behind.

Ridge Field

The young man crossed over a low hill and onto an **expansive** farm field, stopping only long enough to put the wooden bucket down near men and women who were bent over rows of large green plants with broad leaves. This field of **tobacco** plants, called Ridge Field, stretched very far in the distance. The people there paid the little dog no attention since he stood so close to the ground that the huge leaves covered his fur coat and hat.

One man—older, with a grey beard—spoke to the young man who had brought the bucket full of water, and they smiled at each other. The older man went back to work, and the young man turned and walked quickly away, his pace almost a sprint.

Dachshunds can keep up with humans, but only for a short time. Colonial Klaus hoped that the young man would soon stop so that he could catch his breath. Soon enough, the young man came into a clearing and a woman's voice rang out clearly, "Billy, come here and help me feed the chickens!" The little dog then saw a little house made of wood and clay, with a chimney on one side and a makeshift wooden fence around its **perimeter**, where four or five chickens were walking about to and fro—waiting **impatiently** for their own supper.

The woman met Billy at the gate and handed him some corn, which he threw out to the squawking poultry. Colonial Klaus had hung back watching the scene, but, as Billy was throwing the corn out, he caught sight of the little dog wearing the tri-corn hat. "Mamma—someone has come for a visit!" said Billy in the direction of the open door of the little house.

The Hubbards

"I have no time for that, Billy, I've got to get up to Mr. Jefferson's house to prepare the supper!"
And with that the woman disappeared around the back of the house, and headed away from them.

The young man turned towards Klaus. "Don't worry about her—that's my mamma, Hannah, and I'm Billy Hubbard," said the young man to Colonial Klaus. "You have a fine hat and feather, I see, but it's a little out of date. People don't wear those hats anymore—only Mr. Jefferson, because he prefers the old style of clothes from when he was a young man during the Revolutionary days."

Klaus remembered Mr. Jefferson's mentioning the 'Spirit of '76' and knew this must have been an important moment in time. But he still wasn't sure what it was about.

As he was thinking, Klaus was taking in the room around him and Billy was watching him do it. The room contained very little: a rope bed with a **trundle** underneath it, a stool, a long wooden table in front of the fire, and some pegs on the wall, from which hung a shirt and an apron. Billy handed the little dog a piece of **hoecake** left over from the early morning breakfast and then began to tell Klaus about his life.

Billy's voice dropped lower, and the little dog understood that what the young man was about to tell him was equally important as what the 'Spirit of '76' meant to Mr. Jefferson. "I tell you, Colonial Klaus, I don't like living here and I don't like working '**in the ground**' every day from sunup to sundown. One day I'm going to go away from here. It won't be easy, because I'll have to leave my mamma, but I want to be my own man."

The little dog didn't say anything, but his own brown eyes met Billy's brown eyes and he saw that the young man was very serious. Klaus wondered where Billy would go and if he would be safe. As a little dog who had himself once been left at the animal shelter, Klaus was sensitive to what it meant to be alone and scared. A nice man had adopted him and taken him home and away from the loneliness, but would Billy be so fortunate?

Outside the House

Colonial Klaus broke out of his memories when Billy said he had to go back to the tobacco field for more work. The afternoon was wearing on and Billy directed the little dog to a path behind the house—the one Hannah had taken—that would bring him directly to the octagonal house where Mr. Jefferson, Ellen, and Cornelia were waiting for him. Klaus hoped he would see Billy again as he watched the young man head in the opposite direction, back toward Ridge Field.

His nose twitching in the summer air and his stomach growling a bit, the little dog was looking forward to the upcoming meal and meeting Mr. Jefferson and his granddaughters again. He came upon a funny looking fence—it jagged this way and that, like a snake—and he followed along its **interior**.

Rounding a bend, the little dog saw a brick house that seemed much larger than it really was because it sat above him, and he was really very small. The red-brick walls had a contrasting thick white trim across the top and green **shutters**. This house looked very different from Billy's house, but there was only one way to find out—and that was to climb the seven stairs to the front door that sat under a large, long triangle. Dogs don't usually concern themselves with **arithmetic** and geometric shapes—a good bone, walks in the sunshine, and a comfortable place to nap were the things most meaningful to dachshunds—but, Klaus could tell there was something special about this house. It wasn't squared like Billy's house, and it wasn't round like his dog bowl. It was a combination between the two. *What would such a house look like inside?* wondered Klaus. But, again, there was the small problem of the many steps. Steps like these weren't made for short legs. He would have to find another way in.

Hannah's Kitchen

Walking around the house, Klaus was shaded by tall trees with large, broad, green leaves. His nose pulled him forward, the smell of corn cooking and something sweet **luring** him to the back of the octagonal house to an open doorway.

Inside, Klaus could see Hannah, Billy's mother, expertly moving back and forth between a roaring fire in the hearth and a series of small stoves to the side. The little dog kept his distance but noted the long wooden table in front—a meal was taking shape and he certainly didn't want to get in the way.

It took a few moments for Hannah to notice him—the funny little dog sitting in the doorway wearing a wool tri-corn hat—but when she did, she smiled quickly and said, "Don't get in my way, Colonial Klaus! Mr. Jefferson likes his supper exactly at 3 p.m.!"

Klaus nodded his head in assent, and understood then that both Billy and Hannah did not have a choice in their work for Mr. Jefferson. This became clear when the kitchen bell rang and Hannah's pace quickened.

The house and the work in the field ran on Mr. Jefferson's time. Billy and Hannah and the other people he saw in the field each had jobs to do and all did them according to plan.

And, with this **realization**, the little dog knew it was time for him to get upstairs, otherwise he would be late for his invitation. He had a feeling the conversation with Mr. Jefferson would be something he did not want to miss. He had many questions to ask Mr. Jefferson about the house, and the land, and the people who lived there, like Billy and Hannah.

Inside the House

Backing away from his post at the kitchen door, Klaus found another open doorway under three brick arches and stepped inside. It was the basement of the house and was cool and shadowy, and he felt a bit of relief after being in the warm Virginia sun and near the heat of the kitchen.

Out of the corner of his eye, Klaus saw a rope bed with a blue checked **coverlet** tucked under a moon-shaped window. The basement was rather chilly now, and smelled faintly of moss mixed with wine. "Ah, you must be Colonial Klaus!" said a man coming towards the little dog. "I'm Burwell Colbert, Mr. Jefferson's personal servant. That right there is Mr. Jefferson's wine cellar," he said, pointing to the wooden crates stacked in a large open pit close by, "and this is my bed. No time for talking, though, Colonial Klaus. I better get you upstairs. Mr. Jefferson, Miss Ellen, and Miss Cornelia are waiting for you in the library."

And with that, Burwell picked up Klaus and placed him in the **crook** of his left arm (dachshunds are handy like that, you can take them anywhere because they can be carried easily). Burwell headed towards a narrow set of stairs that wound up to the first floor of the octagonal house. "I know all the ways in and out of this place, Colonial Klaus!" said Burwell, and the little dog imagined that he did.

He saw that Burwell was better dressed than Billy, and he was glad for a moment to rest his little body in the crook of Burwell's arm—the long walk across the fields had tired him out.

They reached the first floor of the house and the little dog got a brief view of small rooms and even a bed that seemed to be suspended between two walls. The bed looked very comfortable, but Klaus knew it was not the right time for a nap—nor could he figure out a way of getting up into a bed so high. Sleep would have to wait.

Burwell took Klaus through the next room—which smelled much like a dining room (that, too, would have to wait for the moment)—and into the library, where the sound of voices was heard. Klaus straightened his tri-corn hat and prepared to greet (again) the Jeffersons.

Stories in the Library

Putting Klaus down, Burwell formally introduced him to the room. "This is Colonial Klaus, who has come for a visit and supper, Mr. Jefferson."

As Burwell left, Ellen and Cornelia smiled and welcomed him into the room. Klaus had never really seen a room like it: all along one wall were windows reaching from the floor to the ceiling, open to the outside air, and in between, tall bookcases filled with books of all shapes and sizes. Reading was something that his owner did almost every day, but his owner read books while listening to headphones. These instead were old-fashioned books, with cloth covers and beautiful **marbleized** endpapers inside and pictures, too, which were the little dog's favorite thing about books.

Mr. Jefferson was sitting down in a low, wide chair with short legs that curved to the floor. He had been reading aloud while Ellen and Cornelia worked at their drawings at a circular table nearby. Jefferson looked down at the little dog, and said, "Truthfully, Colonial Klaus, I own a dog at Monticello, but there is something about you that makes me believe your curiosity elevates you above other dogs. That and your tri-corn hat, of course. If you could talk, I wonder what stories you could tell us today."

Klaus did have a story, but how could he tell Mr. Jefferson he had somehow been transported back in time, and more importantly, how would he ever get home? For the time being, he had no answer.

"Would you like me to tell you a little about the Spirit of '76 and why I like your hat so much?" asked Jefferson. "Come sit near me and I'll tell you about the year 1776, when a new nation was formed—but not without great sacrifice."

Jefferson placed a cushion near his chair, Klaus made himself comfortable, and the girls continued their drawing. Ellen and Cornelia had heard their grandfather's stories before, of writing the Declaration of Independence during the hot summer of 1776 in Philadelphia, and of all the fighting between **representatives** from different states about his choice of words and the meaning behind them. But the words had lasted, especially the second stanza, which even Klaus from the twenty-first century **recognized**:

> We hold these truths to be self-evident, that all men are created equal, that they are endowed by their Creator with certain unalienable Rights, that among these are Life, Liberty and the pursuit of Happiness.

Jefferson went on to tell Klaus of living in Paris for five years to establish the new government, and of meeting Alexander Hamilton in New York City. Finally, Jefferson finished by showing Klaus plans for the building of a new college, with a library at its center! These were old stories to Ellen and Cornelia, but to Klaus, each one was more significant than the last.

Burwell then opened the glass doors. "Sirs, your supper is getting cold!" Jefferson's love for punctuality had been abandoned for the Spirit of '76.

The Pursuit of Happiness

Ellen, Cornelia, Mr. Jefferson, and the little dog sat around the dining room table.

"You see, Colonial Klaus, the table is eight sided, just as the house is!" offered Ellen.

Cornelia nodded her head in agreement. "Yes, Grandfather loves octagons—his other house, Monticello, has an octagonal room in it and is much larger, but we like this house better," continued Cornelia.

"Yes, we do," agreed Ellen—"because here grandfather is relaxed and happy. Every night we read together and then sleep in our little beds."

Klaus saw that here in the octagonal house, people were happy, but, if that was the case, why wasn't Billy happy? With a little more thought, he came to the understanding that some people at Poplar Forest were allowed to pursue their happiness, but others, like Billy, Hannah, and Burwell, weren't. This seemed then the biggest difference between where he had come from, and where he was now.

Mr. Jefferson caught the little dog's thoughtful expression. "Yes, it is true, Colonial Klaus. People such as Hannah and Burwell labor for my happiness." The dog watched him hesitate for a moment. "And, though I know it to be **grievously** wrong, I have no solution for it, for I depend on them."

Klaus could see that the subject made Mr. Jefferson a little less **buoyant**, a little less at ease. "Perhaps one day, people will find a way to address this **injurious** state of affairs, but at the moment, we **have the wolf by the ear**."

Ellen and Cornelia had gone quiet and watched their grandfather—perhaps they realized that one day they would inherit all of the Jefferson legacy, good and bad. The candles on the table were lit, as the sun was going down and the skylight above them darkened.

As a dog, Klaus was basically color blind, but he knew that then, as is now, there were contradictions in the way humans acted. This was less so for the canine family. Dogs (and even their cousins, the wolves) had only a few basic needs and these needs were met with some food, a comfortable bed, and a scratch under the chin. The pursuit of happiness was not so straightforward for humans.

The Day is Past and Gone

By the end of the supper made by Hannah—a simple, delicious meal of summer vegetable stew and bread, chocolate from a chocolate pot, and just a wee bit of the wine from Mr. Jefferson's cellar—everyone around the table was **satiated** and ready for an evening walk.

"Please join us on the **terras**, Colonial Klaus, for some fresh air. The insects will be gone, and our friends the bats will be dancing above our heads."

Klaus thought this a bit strange, to be walking with bats flying around above his head, but he did need some fresh air. And besides, his head was so low to the ground that the bats would never reach him (the bats would definitely reach Mr. Jefferson's head first, but Klaus kept his tri-corn hat on just the same).

Ellen, Cornelia, Mr. Jefferson, and Klaus stepped onto the roof of the wing of offices and could smell Hannah's kitchen below, mixed with the scent of tobacco. Burwell could be seen nearby, leaning against a tree and smoking a white clay tobacco pipe.

It was a quiet, gentle evening. The group walked slowly from one end to the other and back again. An owl let out a soft "hoo, hoo" from one of the poplar trees in the distance.

"I think, my friend, you'll want to stay here for the evening, as it's too late to head back into Lynchburg-town," Mr. Jefferson noted. "Why don't you use that cushion in the library and settle yourself by the fireplace?"

Klaus could hardly disagree. He had seen and learned so much in one day that his eyes were beginning to droop and his paws were a bit **achy**, as was his long back.

Back inside the house, Burwell ushered the little dog into the library, **plumping** up the cushion and stoking the fire. The last thing the little dog remembered was Burwell closing the glass doors behind him, moving off to the next room to help Mr. Jefferson settle in for the evening before retiring to his own bed in the basement.

Back in Lynchburg-town

Klaus gradually awoke and stretched his little body out from nose to tail. Around him the room seemed familiar. Mr. Jefferson, Ellen, Cornelia, Burwell, Billy, and Hannah were nowhere to be seen. Nor was the octagonal house with its tall windows and glass doors.

He was back in his old room with his old owner, who slept peacefully next to him under the curved ceiling of their little house, which was definitely not an octagon, but a two-over-four–room square called a "Cape."

This man, whom people called Jeff, then awoke, too. "O.K., buddy, time to get moving! Another day to work."

Klaus looked at him a bit grumpily—no courtly manners this one!—but he was happy to see him and gave him a lick on the chin with his little pink tongue.

"Thanks, buddy!" Jeff said, with a scratch under the chin.

Klaus realized he was no longer "Colonial Klaus" to others, just plain old Klaus, or "Buddy" as Jeff liked to call him for a nickname.

His owner got out of bed and began to dress for work, leaving Klaus to his thoughts. It was hard to know what happened the day before— was it a dream, were the history books that Jeff always listened to **influencing** his thoughts? Or did his travel to the past really happen?

"Is this your hat buddy?" asked Jeff, picking up a grey tri-corn hat from one of the **bedposts**.

And, there it was, the grey wool tri-corn hat with the feather in its brim that had taken him to the past and back.

"Pretty nice hat, Klaus!" said Jeff as he left the room.

Pretty nice hat, indeed! thought the little dog.

THE END

achy— feeling tired and affected with aches

acquaintance— a person someone knows slightly

allée— a walkway lined with trees or shrubs

ancestry— a person's ancestors (a person from whom someone is descended)

arithmetic— a science that deals with the addition, subtraction, multiplication, and division of numbers

assent— to agree to, or to approve of something

bedpost— any one of the four main supporting posts at each corner of an old-fashioned bed

buoyant— lighthearted or cheerful

coverlet— bedspread

crook— a curved or hooked part of a thing

dachshund— a breed of dogs of German origin with a long body, very short legs, and long drooping ears

discern— to perceive by sight or some other sense

expansive— extending far and wide

geometric— consisting of points, lines, and angles

grievous— serious or grave

have the wolf by the ear— to be in a dangerous situation from which one cannot disengage, but in which one cannot safely remain. Thomas Jefferson used this phrase several times in his letters, and it refers to the institution of slavery, where whites understood slavery to be wrong, but, were afraid of the consequences of freeing thousands of enslaved people of color. In one letter from 1820, he writes:

But, as it is, we have the wolf by the ear, and we can neither hold him nor safely let him go. Justice is in one scale, and self-preservation in the other.

hoecake— a small cornmeal cake

immobile— unable to move or be moved

impatient— not wanting to put up with or wait for something or someone

in the ground—Thomas Jefferson's term for an enslaved person who was sent to work in the plantation fields

influence— to cause or encourage (a person) to do something

injurious— causing injury or harm

interior— being or occurring inside something

intoxicate— to excite to enthusiasm

lure— to attract or tempt

marbleized— having a finish like that of a marble (swirling patterns of color)

peaked— looking pale and sick

pedigree— a list showing the line of ancestors of a person or animal

perimeter— the border or outer boundary of an area

plantation fare— a kind of food, here referring to the foods prepared on and for those living on plantations, a large area of land where crops are grown and harvested

plump— to make or become round or filled out

realization— the act of becoming aware of something

recognize— to know and remember upon seeing

representatives— people elected to act for others

reverie— the state of being lost in thought, especially about pleasant things

Revolutionary (War)— of, or relating to, the American Revolution, the war in which the American colonies broke free from Great Britain and became a new country (1775–1783)

satiate— to satisfy fully or to excess

shutter— a usually movable cover for the outside of a window

terras— Thomas Jefferson used this word to mean terrace, or a raised place to walk next to a building. Jefferson built these above the wings of offices at both Monticello and Poplar Forest.

tobacco— a tall upright tropical American herb with pink or white flowers that is grown for its leaves. Tobacco was grown on many of Thomas Jefferson's plantations, as the leaves were used for pipe smoking— especially popular in England.

trundle— a low bed on small wheels that can be rolled under a taller bed

visitant— Thomas Jefferson used the words "curious visitants" in a letter to his daughter Martha Jefferson Randolph to describe the day, November 4, 1815, when Andrew Jackson and his traveling companions stopped at Poplar Forest to see him and the house:

I was most agreeably surprised to find that the party whom I thought to be merely curious visitants were General Jackson and his suite, who passing on to Lynchburg did me the favor to call.

The definitions provided here were drawn from the Merriam-Webster Dictionary. In the early 1800s, a man named Noah Webster from Connecticut spent more than two decades writing the first comprehensive dictionary for the United States. Webster corresponded with Thomas Jefferson—a series of letters between Jefferson and Webster dated to the 1790s still exists in the National Archives in Washington, D.C.! Two years after Thomas Jefferson's death, Noah Webster published his An American Dictionary of the English Language. Even though Jefferson and Webster differed in their political views, Jefferson would surely have admired Webster's word-based project, which helped to shape American language and culture.

Burwell Colbert (1783—1862; pronounced "Burl")

Colbert was born into slavery, and spent his youth at the nailery on Mulberry Row at Monticello, and also learned to paint and glaze windows. His work was seen in painting the Chinese railing at Monticello and also Jefferson's carriage. As an adult he was Thomas Jefferson's manservant—with him all the time, and traveling with him from Monticello to Poplar Forest and back. Colbert was recognized by Thomas Jefferson and those around him and given freedoms not granted to most enslaved persons, such as traveling to town when he wanted, and purchasing his own clothes, made possible by the twenty dollars Jefferson gave to him annually. From two wives—his first wife was enslaved and his second wife, a free woman of color—Colbert became father to eleven children. A member of the extended Hemings family, Colbert was one of only five people freed when Thomas Jefferson died. His burial site is unknown.

Hannah Hubbard (1770— unknown death date)

Though born at Monticello, Hannah Hubbard moved to Poplar Forest and, as an adult, became the cook, housekeeper and washer woman for Thomas Jefferson and his family, when they visited several times a year. Hannah was married twice and had many children, one of whom, Billy Hubbard, was eventually sold, due to his continual acts of resistance against enslavement. From surviving letters and a few pieces of material culture found during archaeological excavations, it is known that Hannah could read and write—an unusual skill for an enslaved person in Virginia. Hannah was also devoutly Christian, and may have gone to church at the nearby African Meeting House in Forest. She is last mentioned in a provisions list from 1821. The contours of her life afterward are unknown.

William "Billy" Hubbard (1799— unknown death date)

Born at Poplar Forest, Billy was sent to Monticello to learn a trade on Mulberry Row, the area on the Monticello plantation where enslaved people lived and worked. As a young man Billy began rebelling against his enslavement, angering those around him, and Jefferson had Billy removed from the shops at Monticello and sent to the fields to work at Poplar Forest. At age 20 Billy attacked an overseer (a farm manager on a plantation who was responsible for the work of enslaved people), which he did again three years later, prompting Jefferson to sell him after punishment by whipping and having his hand burned. Billy ended up in Louisiana where he rebelled again, and was sold again. Nothing is known about him afterward.

Thomas Jefferson (1743—1826)

Born on his father's plantation called Shadwell in 1743, Thomas was the first son of Peter and Jane Jefferson, and therefore he inherited thousands of acres of land and hundreds of enslaved people when his father died. Thomas went to the College of William & Mary and studied to become a lawyer, serving in the Virginia House of Burgesses (government). He became a member of the Continental Congress and wrote the Declaration of Independence during the summer of 1776 in Philadelphia. Afterward, Jefferson went on to become governor of Virginia, Secretary of State under George Washington, Vice President under John Adams, and finally President of the United States for two terms, 1801—1809.

In addition to his political work, Jefferson was an avid gardener, inventor, architect, and reader. He designed Monticello, his primary home, his retreat house, Poplar Forest and the University of Virginia. Enslaved people lived and worked at both plantations and the school, including the Hemingses. Jefferson's wife died in 1782 after ten years of marriage, and eventually Jefferson would have a relationship with Sally Hemings, an enslaved house maid, fathering six children with her. Jefferson died on the same day as John Adams, July 4, 1826, when the country was celebrating the 50th anniversary of the Declaration of Independence. He is buried at Monticello.

Ellen Wayles Randolph (1796—1876)

Ellen, born Eleonora, was one of Thomas Jefferson's grandchildren from his daughter Martha Jefferson Randolph. When visiting Poplar Forest from Monticello, Jefferson often took Ellen and her sister Cornelia with him for company. Ellen may have been a favorite with her grandfather because she was a scholar and a linguist, although as a woman she was allowed to practice her skills only in her own home. She married Joseph Coolidge and moved to Boston, Massachusetts where she had six children. She is buried at the famous Mount Auburn Cemetery in Cambridge.

Cornelia Jefferson Randolph (1799—1871)

Three years younger than her sister Ellen, Cornelia was equally talented, especially in the area of the arts. Her grandfather Thomas Jefferson provided her with the materials to learn architectural drawing, and she often copied images of the University of Virginia as Jefferson was working. Because she did not marry, Cornelia lived with her brother, and later sisters, and ran an art school out of her brother's home, close to Monticello, called Edgehill. She taught drawing, painting, and sculpture, and a beautiful bust of her in terra cotta still exists in the collections of Monticello. She visited Poplar Forest often with her grandfather and sister, and also visited Natural Bridge with them in 1817. Although Cornelia died in Alexandria, she was buried at Monticello.

Acknowledgements

Thomas Jefferson's Poplar Forest gratefully thanks all of the donors who contributed to the online sprint campaign for the print production of *Colonial Klaus* and especially the following individuals and organizations including:

Mary C. Armstrong,
National President's Project, 2018—2021, National Society Daughters of the American Colonists

Dr. Genevieve Neale,
Pawprints Mobile Medicine for Pets

Suzanne Innes

Evelyn Kinkade

Paul and Alexandra Macaluso

Missouri State Society Daughters of American Colonists

**Aux Arcs Chapter
MSS DAC/NSDAC**

The origins of "Colonial Klaus" came from Kyle Tello and Jeffrey Nichols, who created the time-traveling dog by placing a tri-corn hat and "Ben Franklin" glasses on the real-life Klaus, posing him for a photo in the house. Later, a stuffed dachshund given to Thomas Jefferson's Poplar Forest from Pawprints Mobile Medicine for Pets, again wearing the hat and glasses, became a mascot at the front desk. Friends and staff showed great interest in the project, including Kate Jenkins of The History Press and Sarah, Claire, and Maegan Ramsey, who all read the first draft. Thank you to Rachel Honchul, Mary Massie, and Gail Pond for reviewing the manuscript, and to Bill Barker for allowing us to use his image. Thanks also to the work of museum staff—the archaeologists, administrators, educators, and preservationists—at Monticello and Poplar Forest who have worked for decades to excavate the story of the enslaved communities at both plantation sites, and to all Jefferson scholars who continue to refine our knowledge about the man and his legacy. Many thanks to Nancy Marion of Blackwell Press, for the excellent editing, design, and production of the original text.

About the Author & Illustrator

LAURA A. MACALUSO, PH.D. is the author of books and essays about art and history, with a focus on monuments, material culture, and museums. Her recent publications include *The Public Artscape of New Haven: Themes in the Creation of a City Image*, *A Guide to Thomas Jefferson's Virginia*, and *Monument Culture: International Perspectives on the Future of Monuments in a Changing World*. She also contributed the essay "Public Art Inside and Outside the Museum" to *State of Museums: Voices from the Field*. She has taught art history classes at the college level, and works as a grant writer for art organizations in Virginia, New York, and Connecticut. She loves art, books, traveling, the Beatles, the bunnies and birds living in her backyard, the Blue Ridge Mountains, and her family and friends, whether they be animal or human.

LYNDEN A. GODSOE was raised alongside the ponies, dogs, and cats of her family's horseback riding facility in West Grove, Pennsylvania, brought up in the middle of two sisters, each with talents of their very own. It was her homeschool upbringing and rural lifestyle that has inspired a thoughtful, imaginative life, and a blossoming collection of illustrative work. Her work captures the imaginative side of nature that she has carried with her from her recreational and nature classes with her family amongst the fields and streams of White Clay Creek, and the "Wyeth country" that she feels home to. Her characters, both human and animals, convey a thoughtfulness in their activities. Usually, all seem to be pondering or simply enjoying life. It can be revealed by some who look closely—there is more to them than first meets the eye.